For Nick

With love – M.E.

EGMONT
We bring stories to life

First published 2011
by Egmont UK Limited
239 Kensington High Street, London W8 6SA

ISBN HB 978 1 4052 4811 2
ISBN PB 978 1 4052 4812 9

A CIP catalogue record for this title is available
from The British Library

1 3 5 7 9 10 8 6 4 2

Printed in China

Poggle

and the Treasure

MICHAEL EVANS

EGMONT

Poggle and his best friend, Henry
were digging a hole on the beach.

"Hey!" spluttered Poggle.
"You're throwing sand over my head."

"Whoops, sorry," said Henry.

They had spent the day
playing pirates.

They'd made a pirate ship.

Eaten a pirate lunch.

And fought a scary sea monster.

Now they were digging for buried treasure.

Clunk!

"It's treasure, it's treasure!" cried Henry.

Poggle scraped away the sand to reveal . . .

...an egg!

"Oh," said Henry.

"I wonder what's inside?" said Poggle.

"Come out!"

Henry shouted.

"We want to see you."

"That won't work," said Poggle.
"We need to keep it warm. "

"I could sit on it - like a hen," Henry said helpfully.

"You'd break it," said Poggle. "I'll fetch
something cosy from home,
then we can wait for it
to come out."

And off he ran.

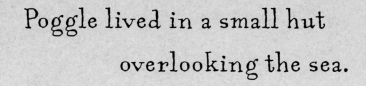

Poggle lived in a small hut
overlooking the sea.

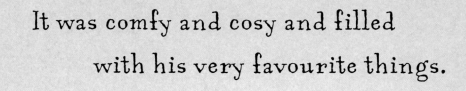

It was comfy and cosy and filled
with his very favourite things.

He found a snuggly scarf,
and ran back to the beach.

"There we are," said Poggle,
wrapping the scarf around the egg.
"Now we just have to wait until it opens."

And so they waited.

And waited.

And waited.   Until . . .

Crack!

. . . the egg
began to open.

"What if it's not friendly?" whispered Henry.

"It might have big pointy teeth," said Poggle. "And sharp, scratchy claws."

They both began to feel a bit frightened.

Crack . . . Crack . . . Crack!

"Look out," said Poggle. "It's coming!"

"Hide!" said Henry.

And they jumped into the sandy hole.

The cracking noises continued.

And then . . . silence.

Poggle nudged Henry. "Have a look."

"No! You look," said Henry.

So Poggle bravely stood up and peeked over the top of the hole.

There on the sand sat a small creature.

"Well, it doesn't look scary," said Poggle.

Henry stood up. "Hello, what's your name?"

The creature didn't answer.

"It's only a baby," giggled Poggle.

"Goo goo gaa gaa," said Henry.

"I bet he's hungry," said Poggle, and he ran off to get some milk from his hut.

The creature sniffed it, smiled and began to slurp.

When all the milk was gone the creature began to shuffle away.

"I wonder where he's going?" said Henry.

"Let's follow him," said Poggle.

But then the little thing tripped
and fell down a sand dune.

"Oh no!"

cried Poggle and Henry
together.

At the bottom of the hill, Poggle carefully
lifted the creature up.

"Are you all right?" asked Henry.

"He's fine," said Poggle.

Poggle slowly put the creature down on the sand,
and it began to shuffle away to the sea.

As soon as it got to the shore,
it stood on tiptoes and began waving.

"What's it doing?" asked Poggle.
Henry pointed. "Look, it's waving to its Mummy."

The creature gave them a huge smile.

Then with a splish and a splash it was gone.

"He was nice," said Henry waving.

"Yes," said Poggle,
"a *real* treasure."

And Poggle and Henry
ran back up the beach to see what else
they could find.